★ ~~HOPELESS~~

PROBLEMS WITH
PYTHAGORAS!

STELLA
TARAKSON

Sweet
Cherry

Published by Sweet Cherry Publishing Limited
Unit 36, Vulcan House,
Vulcan Road,
Leicester, LE5 3EF
United Kingdom

First published in the UK in 2018
2020 edition

4 6 8 10 9 7 5 3

ISBN: 978-1-78226-348-7

© Stella Tarakson

Hopeless Heroes: Problems with Pythagoras!

Cover design by Nick Roberts and Rhiannon Izard
Illustrations by Nick Roberts

www.sweetcherrypublishing.com

Printed and bound in Turkey
T.IO006

For my daughter, Connie,

for believing that I could

'I've got the results of last week's maths test.' Miss Omiros picked a sheaf of papers off her desk and strode around the classroom, her high heels tapping. 'Most people did well. Ajay came first as usual. Full marks, well done.' The teacher smiled as she handed Ajay his test paper.

From across the room, Tim glimpsed a gigantic *A* written in red. He gave his best friend a thumbs up. Ajay suppressed a grin. He tried to look modest, but by the way his dark eyes gleamed, Tim knew he was feeling smug.

'Leo had the biggest improvement.' Miss Omiros walked towards Tim's desk, which he unfortunately shared with his worst enemy, Leo the bully. Miss Omiros thought that making Leo sit closer to the front would improve his behaviour. As if! She handed Leo his test paper, which had a big (written on it. 'An improvement from last time. Keep up the good work.'

Leo usually looked stony faced when he got his marks, but now his pale lips twitched into a smile. It transformed his bull-like features into something almost human.

Miss Omiros paused in front of Tim. 'So … what happened there? This isn't like you.' Frowning, she handed over his paper.

Tim's eyebrows shot to the top of his forehead as he glanced at his mark.

An F.

F! A flood of heat rushed into his cheeks. Sure, maths wasn't his best subject, but he usually did well enough. In his whole life, he'd never, ever–

'HAH! LOSER!'

Leo crowed gleefully as soon as the teacher moved on. 'Who's the smart one now, Cinderella?'

Wincing at the sound of his nickname, Tim flipped the paper over with a snap, hiding the mark. He hated being called Cinderella. Just because he did the housework. He couldn't help it: Mum worked two jobs and he was expected to help out. And now this!

'I had a bad day. That's all.' Tim

shrugged as if he didn't care.

'I beat you. You probably came last.'

'Leo, that's enough,' Miss Omiros said from across the room. 'Don't spoil a good day by being unpleasant.'

The bully fell silent, but he leered as he made a giant L with his thumb and forefinger and held it against his freckled forehead.

L for loser. F for failure. Tim felt a prickle in the corners of his eyes and blinked. He knew why his marks were bad. He hadn't concentrated during the test. His mind was too full. What with his friend Hercules being upset with him, and with Mr Green turning out to be Mum's boyfriend ...

It was all too much.

Tim still hadn't recovered from the shock of discovering that a teacher at his school was seeing Mum. Not that he disliked Mr Green – or Larry, as he was told to call him. A laid-back Australian, most kids considered him cool. But it's one thing to chat to a teacher in the playground, and quite another to have him sitting in your kitchen making goo-goo eyes at your mother.

The getting-to-know-each-other dinner last week had been awkward. Tim hadn't wanted to say the wrong thing, so he'd said very little. Mum had kept flashing him anxious looks. It was clear she wanted everyone to get along. Tim tried to smile and act happy, but he'd still been reeling from the fallout of his latest adventure in Ancient Greece. Tim had returned to his own time ... in disgrace. Although he'd looked regretful, Hercules had ordered Tim to go home and never return.

Tim hadn't meant to put the hero's daughter in danger! He and Zoe had decided to rescue a gorgon's victims – people who'd been turned to stone by the monster's glance.

They'd succeeded,
but Hercules had
banned Zoe from
going on adventures
ever again. He'd
even confiscated the

MAGIC VASE

that allowed Tim to travel
through time.

Tim understood. Hercules
was only trying to protect Zoe. It
still hurt though.

Forcing the feeling from his mind, Tim
frowned at his maths paper. Where had
he gone wrong? Numbers swam before
his eyes, blurring and bumping into each

other. They refused to make sense. He needed help.

An idea struck and he sat up straight. He could ask Mr Gr– Larry! Everyone said the teacher was a maths whizz. Then Tim could tell Mum that they were getting along well and she'd be relieved. He'd kill two birds with one stone: help with maths and a happy mother!

The bell rang and everyone jumped up, scraping their chairs against the floor. Tim spotted Larry in the playground, surrounded by a group of children.

Tim hadn't spoken to him since the night of the dinner, unsure what he should say to the man. A school trip to the British Museum was coming up, and

Larry was one of the teachers that would be going. Tim had been worried that it would be awkward, but now he felt as if the problem were sorted. He ran up to him and grinned shyly. The teacher smiled back.

'Hi Mr ... err ... Larry.'

The kids giggled when they heard him use the teacher's first name.

The smile froze on the man's face. 'Not here,' he muttered so that only Tim could hear. 'Don't call me Larry here.'

'Sorry! I meant Mr Green.'

'That's better. What can I do for you, mate?' The teacher sounded friendly, but he was talking to Tim like he would to any other kid in the school.

'Well, um …' Tim looked at the sea of faces, suddenly uncertain. Maybe this wasn't such a good idea. Were Mum and Mr Green meant to be a secret? He vaguely recalled her saying that, but he'd been too busy fretting about Hercules to pay much attention.

'Yes?'

Tim had to be careful not to mention his mother. 'I was hoping you'd help me with my maths.'

Mr Green squinted down at him. 'Is there any reason your teacher can't help? Miss Omiros, isn't it?'

'Yes. But I got a bad mark in my test and–'

'Sorry, mate. I'm sure Miss Omiros will help you.'

The children looked at Tim as if he'd sprouted an extra head. Confused, he turned away, shoulders slumped. That hadn't gone well. Maybe talking to Mr Green at school was a mistake. But how was he supposed to treat him? Like a friend or like a stranger? And shouldn't Mr Green *want* to help him? The teacher was coming over for dinner tonight, too. What if he told Mum about Tim's request for help? What if Mum got cross at Tim?

NOTHING WAS SIMPLE ANYMORE!

If only he had someone to talk to, someone who could tell him what stepfathers were meant to be like. He didn't want to upset Mum by complaining about Larry. And he couldn't tell Ajay, not if the relationship was meant to be a secret. The only person he could confide in lived thousands of years ago, in Ancient Greece. And Tim wasn't supposed to be able to go back.

Except … thanks to a trick played on Hercules by the god Hermes, Tim actually *could* go back if he wanted to. The question was: Should he?

Or would that make things worse?

Tim wasn't too sure about Hermes. Could the messenger god – who was also the god of thieves and liars – be trusted? Unknown to Hercules, Hermes had swapped the confiscated vase with a fake copy. It looked exactly the same but it had no powers. He gave

19

Hercules the copy and gave the magical vase back to Tim. He told Tim to use it to return to Ancient Greece whenever he liked.

So maybe the god was trying to be nice. OR DID HE HAVE ANOTHER MOTIVE?

Hermes served Hera, Hercules' deadliest enemy. With a hatred born of jealousy, the angry goddess had once trapped the hero inside the magic vase. It was only when Tim

accidentally broke
the vase that the hero was
set free. Did Hera want Tim
to have the vase so that
she could use him to trap
Hercules again? It would be a
lot harder for her to take it from the
hero himself, Tim guessed. Hercules
would – hopefully! – take precautions.

All week long, Tim had felt torn.
Should he go back to Ancient Greece or
shouldn't he? Would Hercules accept his
apology or refuse to see him? If only
Larry– Mr Green … had turned out to be
nicer. He might have been someone to go
to for advice. But no. The teacher couldn't

even be bothered to help Tim with maths. It showed how much he cared!

Dinner that night turned out to be even more awkward than the first time. At least Mr Green – who, confusingly, was now to be called Larry again – hadn't mentioned Tim's request for help. Not yet, anyway.

Tim picked at his food.

His mother asked him what was wrong.

'Don't you like your roast, dear? Usually you ask for seconds.'

'I'm not hungry.' Tim pushed the parsnip around his plate. He remembered how ravenous Hercules always seemed to be, and sighed.

'Not hungry? Are you feeling sick?'

'A bit,' he admitted. He was. In a way.

Mum leaned over and placed
a cool hand on his forehead.
'You don't have a fever. Maybe
something you ate disagreed with
you.'

Tim started to nod, but froze when
Larry spoke.

'Or is something upsetting you?'

You are, is what Tim felt like saying, but didn't. Instead, he shrugged.

'Is there something wrong?' Mum asked, glancing from her boyfriend to her son.

'I – I failed my maths test.' Tim avoided looking at Larry.

'Really? That's not like you!' Mum's face creased with concern.

The teacher patted Tim on the shoulder. 'No worries, mate. Everyone fails sometimes. Work harder and you'll be right.'

'Can't you help him, Larry? Maths is your forté.' Head tilted to the side, Mum gave her boyfriend a beaming smile. 'I'm sure Tim will be grateful.'

Larry shook his head. 'I don't think it's right. It'd be favouritism.'

Mum's smile faded and her eyes lost some of their shine. 'It's hardly favouritism. You're not his teacher, so how can it be? All I'm saying is spend a few minutes going over what he got wrong. No one will know.'

'I'll know,' Larry said. 'Tim will know. We should start as we mean to go on.'

'So this is how you plan to go on! By ignoring my son when he has a problem!'

Uh oh. Now they were starting to fight. Because of him.

'Look, Penny, I think you're making too big a deal of this.'

Mum's eyes flashed. 'Is that so? I'm sorry that you feel that way!'

Whimpering, Tim pushed back his chair. Could things get any worse? He got up from the table and fled to his room, Mum's voice ringing in his ears.

▪ ▪ ▪

Tim opened his wardrobe door and pulled out the vase. It was still draped in a sheet, even though there was no longer a need to keep it hidden. Not from Hermes, anyway. If the messenger god wanted to steal the vase, he wouldn't have given it to Tim in the first place. Even so, Tim didn't want Mum to see it. She'd only start asking awkward questions about its appearance. Last time Tim was in Greece, Hermes had magically fixed all the cracks that had criss-crossed over the vase. Now it looked as good as new.

Blinking furiously, Tim stared at the vase. He was so tempted to go back. Maybe Hercules had reconsidered the banishment. He might be missing Tim and feeling bad about things. Zoe would be.

If Tim went back, he could talk to the

hero about Larry. Hercules was a good father. He would know what to do.

Mum's footsteps came pattering up the stairs. A second, heavier set of footsteps followed. Any moment now they'd burst into his room. They'd want to talk to him. Tim couldn't face it. Not yet. But would the vase even work? Maybe Hermes had lied and this one was the fake!

Tim's brain was in turmoil. It didn't know what to do, so it let his body decide.

His hands clasped the vase. They held on tight. As if from a distance, Tim heard his own voice squeak out, 'Oh vase, take me to Zoe's house.'

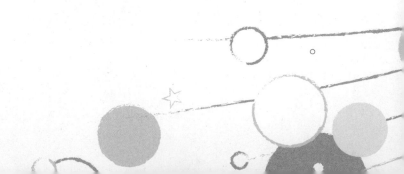

The next thing he knew he was flying through the air, golden sparks shimmering around him.

Tim felt himself land. His eyes, which
he had clamped shut during the flight,
snapped open. Yes! He was standing on
Hercules' doorstep! Hermes hadn't lied.
The vase worked. Tim eased it gently to
the ground then lifted his hand to knock.
Halfway there, he paused. Was this the
right thing to do?

There was still time to change his mind ...
Except that there wasn't. While Tim

dithered, the front door flew open.

'Tim Baker! What are you doing here?' Hercules frowned down at him. His face was rigid, his expression impossible to read.

Tim gulped and moved in front of the vase, desperately hoping the hero wouldn't notice it. 'I, err. Well, I wanted to …'

The hero's bushy eyebrows met in the middle and his thick beard bristled. 'Did I not expel you from my house? Did I not banish you and order you never to return?'

Tim's hopes that Hercules might have forgiven him withered. Shoulders slumped, he nodded miserably.

'Did I not explain that this was to protect my daughter? Yet here you are, bold as bronze.' The hero raised his

dinner-plate sized hands. He stepped
closer, until he was only inches away.

'AND I AM SO GLAD!'

Laughing, Hercules clutched Tim around
the waist and scooped him high into the air.

Tim felt the air whoosh out of him –
partly from being squeezed,
but mostly in relief.

'I have missed you, my friend! And so has Zoe.' Hercules' eyes took on a hunted look. 'I have not heard the end of it since the day you left. My gods, that child knows how to complain.'

Short of breath, Tim could only nod. He believed it.

Hercules swung Tim through the doorway and deposited him on the courtyard floor. His voice grew sombre. 'You are always welcome in my home, Tim Baker. You are a good friend and I regret sending you away. But first you must do something: in the name of Zeus, king of all the gods, promise not to place my daughter in danger again. Are you prepared to make this vow?'

'I promise I'll do everything I can to keep her safe,' Tim replied, looking Hercules in the eye. 'She's my friend and I care about her. But it won't be easy. She doesn't always listen to me.'

The hero was silent for a moment, then nodded. 'This is the truth of the matter. Zoe listens to nobody.' He sighed. 'It is easier to hold up the sky than to keep her at home.'

'Is she here now?' Tim asked, looking around. The house was way too quiet.

'She's at the well with her mother. At least no harm can befall her there.'

Suddenly a flurry of footsteps came along the path. Zoe hurled herself through the open door. Her ringlets bounced and her eyes shone. 'Tim! You're here! I'm so glad you're back.'

Tim glowed with happiness. It was good to be missed.

'Where's your mother?' Hercules asked.

'Still at the well, talking to her friends. I got bored and left. On my way home I saw Tim's vase outside and ran back as fast as I could!'

Tim jumped as a thought hit him. 'Hey! We should bring it in before Hera sees it.' He couldn't forget the goddess' constant threats to trap Hercules in the vase again.

'I'll get it.' Zoe wrestled the amphora into her arms and staggered back, kicking the door shut behind her. The difficulty of grappling with the heavy vase wasn't

enough to wipe the smile off her face
though. Tim helped her carry it through
the courtyard and into the house.

'How about there?' He pointed to a
dark corner.

They put the vase down and Zoe
draped a cloth over it. 'That should do it.'
She beamed at Tim, and then her grin was
replaced by a puzzled frown. 'But – but,
how did you come back? Dad took the
vase away from you.'

Tim didn't want to mention what
Hermes had done. Not within earshot of

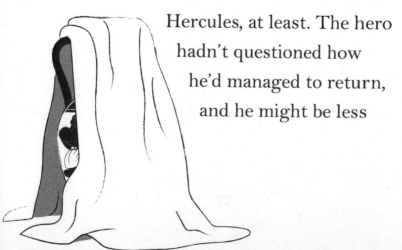 Hercules, at least. The hero
hadn't questioned how
he'd managed to return,
and he might be less

forgiving if he realised he'd been tricked.
'Tell you later,' he said. 'But first I need
your advice. I've got a problem.'

'A problem, my friend?' Hercules said,
following them inside. 'Not that putrid
little bully again! Is he still bothering you?'

'A bit,' Tim admitted, remembering
the L shape that Leo had made with his
fingers. 'But it's not that. It's something
else. Something worse.' He perched on a
hard wooden seat and paused to gather his
thoughts.

'What's wrong?' Zoe sat next to him
and gave his arm a sympathetic squeeze.

'It's my mother.' Tim paused again.

'Did something happen? Is she hurt?'
Zoe prompted.

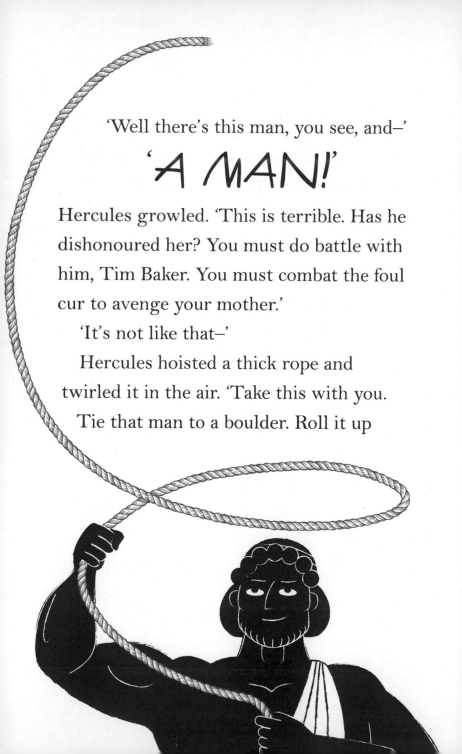

'Well there's this man, you see, and–'

'*A MAN!*'

Hercules growled. 'This is terrible. Has he dishonoured her? You must do battle with him, Tim Baker. You must combat the foul cur to avenge your mother.'

'It's not like that–'

Hercules hoisted a thick rope and twirled it in the air. 'Take this with you. Tie that man to a boulder. Roll it up

the highest mountain. Then call upon
the mightiest eagles to peck out the eyes
that dared to rest upon your mother!' He
dumped the rope in Tim's lap. It was so
heavy Tim slid off the seat.

Picking himself up, Tim let the rope
thump to the floor. 'You've got it wrong.
He's not hurting her. He's her boyfriend.'

'Her what?' the hero barked.

'Her' – Tim groped for the right word –
'suitor.'

'Suitor. I see. So what is the problem? Is
he not worthy?'

'That's just it. I don't know.' Tim kicked
at the rope with his feet. 'He refused to
help me with my maths.'

'He did what?!' Hercules' eyes

narrowed. 'Then I was right. Take the rope, my friend. Use it well.'

'I can't–'

'Then I shall do it!' Hercules pulled himself to his full height. 'Take me with you, Tim Baker. Back to your home. I will soon put an end to this.'

'No!' Tim yelped. 'That's not necessary! Mum likes him. She's happy.'

'So what do you want us to do?' Zoe asked gravely, her hands folded in her lap. 'How can we help?'

Tim shook his head. He wasn't really sure. 'I think I just need some advice. Is he a good man or isn't he? How do I know?'

'Worry not, my friend. This is easily solved.' Hercules picked up a massive pair of sandals that were leaning against the wall. 'I shall come with you. I shall put this suitor to the test. Have I ever mentioned my twelve labours?'

Zoe rolled her eyes. 'Many times.'

'Good. I shall put this man through his own set of labours.' Grunting, Hercules bent down and pulled on the sandals. 'By what name is he known?'

'Larry– Mr Green.'

Hercules lifted his chin. 'So. These trials shall be called "the Labours of Larry Mr Green".'

'That's not necessary,' Tim hastened to say.

Hercules continued as if he hadn't spoken. 'First I shall find some dirty stables for him to clean. Do you know of any? Then I will find a monster for him to fight – the deadlier the better. And then ...'

Tim's spirits sank as Hercules rambled on and on.

He had the feeling he'd just made an awful mistake.

Tim didn't want to hurt the hero's feelings by refusing his offer of help. Not after they'd just made up. But he couldn't let Hercules put Larry through a series of dangerous trials! Mum wouldn't like it. Besides, throwing teachers to monsters was probably against school rules. He flashed Zoe a desperate look.

Zoe gave him a knowing smile. 'That's a great idea. Dad, I think you should go with Tim and help him.'

That's not what Tim meant at all!

'Oh but I …'

'Don't worry about me,' Zoe added. 'I've got plenty of things to keep me occupied.'

The triumphant grin slid off Hercules' face. 'What sort of things?' he asked worriedly. 'Cooking, weaving – those sorts of things?'

'Yes. And … err … other things.' She winked at Tim.

'You are not planning anything dangerous, are you?'

'Not *too* dangerous. Don't worry, I'll be okay.' Zoe held her chin up high.

Hercules stared uneasily at his daughter, then tugged off his sandals. 'Tim Baker, if you do not object, I am needed here. Sorry if I have let you down, my friend.'

'That – that's fine.' Trying to sound crestfallen, he thanked Zoe with a nod. 'I understand. Maybe you could give me some advice instead?'

'Of course!'

Tim hesitated. How could he put his question into words? He barely remembered his own father. All he had were vague memories of a strong embrace, the smell of aftershave, and a smile like sunshine. He'd always felt happy in his dad's arms. Happy and safe.

'How do I know if Larry will be a good stepfather? I mean, what should he be like?'

'That's easy to answer.' Hercules counted on his fingers. 'There are three things that a good man must possess: strength, courage, and strength.'

'You said strength twice,' Zoe pointed out.

'That's because strength is the most important!' Hercules boomed. 'Without it, a man is nothing. Could I have wrestled the Wild Boar of Erymanthus without these?' He flexed his biceps, which bulged like watermelons.

'No,' Tim hastened to agree.

'Do you think I could have chased the Ceryneian Hind if my legs were frail and weak?' Hercules said, peering at Tim's skinny ankles. The hero's face crumpled with pity. 'Do not be offended, Tim Baker, but if you ever need a workout, come to me. Something to build your strength up.

We can start with chicken wrestling and work our way up to boulder rolling.'

'Um, one day.' Tim nodded vigorously, hoping the horror didn't show in his face. 'That'd be great. And thanks for your advice. It's good to know.'

'Dad, that reminds me,' Zoe said, as if she'd just been struck by something important. 'There's this huge boulder down the street that's been getting in my way. Could you move it for me?' Her black eyes sparkled.

'What? That little pebble down the street! Hah. Consider it done. See, Tim Baker, this is what good fathers do.' And with two giant strides, the hero was gone.

'Phew.' Zoe wiped mock sweat off her

brow. 'That should keep him busy for a while. I'll tell you one quality you don't want: overprotectiveness.'

Tim grimaced. 'I don't think that's likely with Larry.'

'So how did you get your vase back?' Zoe asked. 'You didn't say.'

Tim explained about Hermes giving Hercules a fake copy. Zoe frowned, not sure what to make of it. Like Tim, she mistrusted the messenger god's motives.

'We'd better hide the copy or Dad will wonder why there are two vases. I'll put it where he never looks – in the washing basket!'

Laughing, Tim helped her find and move the fake vase. 'So what do you think?' he asked, becoming serious again. 'How can you tell if someone's going to be a good dad?'

'Easy!' Zoe rolled her eyes. 'It's if he lets you do whatever you want.'

Tim chuckled. Hercules certainly was over-protective, but that didn't make him a bad father. 'Hmmm. Is there someone we can talk to about it?'

'Well …' Zoe screwed her face up. 'How about Socrates? He's the wisest man in Greece. If anyone knows, it'll be him.'

Tim had heard of the philosopher. For someone to be famous more than two thousand years after he lived, he must have been pretty smart.

'All right. Where do we find him?'

· · ·

Nobody knew where the philosopher was. Nearly everyone they asked looked shifty and beat a hasty retreat. They didn't seem too keen on running into Socrates. Finally they found a teenaged boy who was willing to talk.

'Try the agora,' the teenager advised them. 'He likes strolling around the open space.'

But Tim was worried about the other people's reactions. Why did they all shy away at the mention of the old man's name? Had history got him wrong, somehow?

'Socrates is super smart, right?'

The teenager laughed. 'Sure he is. He

loves pouncing on passers-by and asking thought-provoking questions. Some people can't handle it, but I think he's cool.'

The children thanked the teenager and he loped away. 'Do you know how to get to the agora?' Tim asked Zoe after he'd left.

'It's this way. Let's go.'

'Hey there, little fans.' The voice over Tim's shoulder was familiar. 'Do you need any awesome hero help again?'

Tim spun around. It was Theseus, the vain Minotaur slayer. In an earlier adventure, he'd tried to help them escape from Hera's labyrinth. He'd put more effort into his heroic poses than in doing anything useful, but for some reason, Zoe went all gooey-eyed whenever she saw him.

'Yes please, that would be wonderful.' Her cheeks turned pink.

'So what can I do for you?' The hero flipped back his long blonde fringe. 'Does it involve fighting? Because I should warn you, I've just washed my hair. It wouldn't help anyone if it got messed up by a monster.'

'Tim's mother has a suitor. We're on a quest to discover what makes a good father,' Zoe said.

Theseus beamed. 'That's easy. Above all things, a man must be attractive.' He rummaged around in the leather pouch slung around his waist, pulled out a mirror and pouted at his reflection. 'A noble brow. A firm chin.' He patted down a stray hair.

Tim shifted impatiently. 'Thanks, but–'

'For my heroic deed of the day, I am prepared to give the suitor a makeover,' Theseus said. 'I can give him some tips, show him how to massage olive oil into his scalp for a fine head of hair. No problem at all.'

'No thanks.' Tim decided to nip that in the bud. 'We're on our way to the agora to see Socrates.'

'Pfft,' Theseus snorted. 'As if he knows anything about skincare! Have you seen those wrinkles?'

'Maybe you could escort us? Keep us safe on the journey?' Zoe simpered.

'Good idea! You can count on me – I don't think there are any hair-messing monsters on the way.'

Tim trailed behind the others and tried to block out the hero's babble. He stared moodily at the ground as they walked, not noticing where they were going, until he heard a familiar sound. A yowling, growling sound of pure animal fury. Startled, Tim looked up.

They were passing Hera's temple. The

sound was her vicious flock
of peacocks, beaks wide open,
calling out a warning to their
mistress!

The sound of peacocks was usually followed by the appearance of Hera herself, as Tim knew only too well. Before he could shout out a warning to the others, the queen goddess materialised. The peacocks flocked behind her like obedient guard dogs.

'So you have returned, Timothy Baker.' Hera strode towards them, her ivory gown rippling in the soft summer breeze.

Her black curls framed her milk-white face. The goddess drew close enough so that Tim could see the icy glint in her pale blue eyes. 'Hermes told me you had been banished and yet here you are. Were you unable to stay away?'

Tim gritted his teeth. He wasn't about to explain himself to Hera. Much better to ignore her and be on their way as quickly as possible.

'That's none of your business!' Zoe stamped her foot, her temper instantly flaring. 'Where Tim goes has nothing to do with you.'

'Perhaps,' the goddess purred,

'but it has plenty to do with your father, does it not? Does he know your little friend is here?'

'As a matter of fact he does. And if you must know–'

Tim tugged on Zoe's arm. 'Forget it.'

There was no point arguing with the goddess. 'We should go.'

'Go where, child?'

Hera's gaze didn't waver from Zoe's face. 'Are you seeking another adventure, in defiance of your father's orders?' She clicked her tongue as if disappointed. 'Dearest me, I shall have to put out an alert on the GGG.'

'No!' Tim didn't want Hera to broadcast over the Greek God Grapevine, a warning system that alerted heroes to danger. 'We're not having an adventure.'

'Is that so? Then why are you out with a hero?' Hera jabbed a bony finger at Theseus.

'Isn't it obvious?' The hero looked affronted. 'I'm gorgeous!'

Hera raised an eyebrow. 'You are Theseus, correct? The one who saved the

Athenian youths from the Minotaur.'

'At your service, Your Majesty.' The hero bowed deeply, but not before flicking back his fringe. 'Do you have a heroic task for me?'

'Not right now. Stand back, Theseus,' Hera warned, gesturing for him to move. 'I don't want you getting in the way.'

The hero obediently shuffled to the side.

'No!'

In that split second, Tim knew that something bad was about to happen. At the same instant that Hera raised her hand, Tim reached out to Zoe, trying to push his friend out of the way. But he was too late. Hera clicked her fingers. Theseus stood motionless, an uncomprehending grin plastered across his face. Tim was too far from Zoe and couldn't reach her. Arms outstretched, he felt himself tumble to the ground. Everything seemed to be happening in slow motion.

Except for one thing.

Quick as a flash, a large wooden structure appeared next to him. Frowning, Tim pulled himself to his feet. He didn't know what it was, but the object filled him with dread.

It was taller than a man and tube-shaped. It was made up of round bands of wood stacked on top of each other, like a barrel. Large Greek letters were printed across the bands. They appeared

to form words that ran
from the top of the
cylinder to the bottom,
but Tim had no idea
what they said. It was a
meaningless jumble to
him.

He scratched his
head. The wooden
tube reminded him of
something … but what?

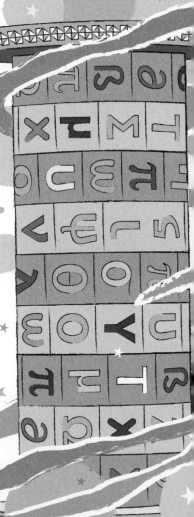

Hera's laughter shattered Tim's thoughts. 'Now go, Timothy Baker. Fetch Hercules. Tell him that if he wants to save his daughter, he must come here and crack the code! Tell him ... tell him it's as *easy as pie*.' With a flash of golden light, Hera and her peacocks disappeared.

Crack the code? Pie? What on earth was the goddess talking about?

'Zoe?' Tim looked around but couldn't see his friend anywhere. Only Theseus, who was smoothing down his hair and straightening his chiton.

'I'm in here!'

With horror, Tim realised her voice was coming from inside the wooden tube. 'Zoe!' He rapped his knuckles on the

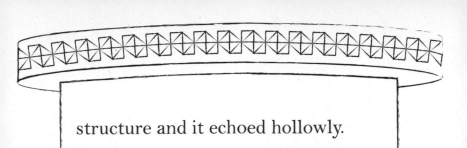

structure and it echoed hollowly.

'Get me out! It's squashy in here.'

Tim walked around it again, this time looking for an entrance. As far as he could tell, there was none. Just the round bands with letters printed on them. Experimenting, he pressed on a letter with the palm of his hand. Nothing. Maybe he needed to push … He pressed hard and the band shifted.

Tim pressed harder. All at once, the band twisted around with a click, its letters moving one place across.

And then, Tim *knew*.

That's why the structure was so familiar!

The large cylinder reminded Tim of the combination lock that he had on his school locker, except that had numbers printed on it instead of letters. To open the lock, you had to twist the little bands of numbers around until they lined up in the right order. So that's what Hera meant by a code. The code was a password, the key to the lock.

Zoe was trapped inside a lock – it was a

puzzle prison!

Tim looked at the strange letters. It would help if he could read Ancient Greek. But even if he could, how could he guess Hera's password? It could be anything!

'Help me figure this out,' he said to Theseus, who was brushing dust off his chiton.

The hero glanced at the giant tube. 'That ugly thing?' he said dismissively. 'It's hardly a fitting tribute to my awesomeness.'

Tim shook his head in despair. 'It's a lock and Zoe's trapped inside,' he said slowly and deliberately. 'We need to solve the puzzle and get her out.'

'Oh. Aren't you good at puzzles?' Theseus asked. 'You solved one for Hercules.'

'That was different; it was a riddle. Anyway, I can't do them in Greek. Only English!'

'What's "English"?'

Tim remembered that he could only talk with Ancient Greek people because of his vase's magic powers. Written on the vase was the spell, 'Those who hold me understand and are understood.'

He was about to try to explain this to Theseus when a barrage of soft thuds came from inside the tube.

'Get me out! Hey!'

Tim could picture Zoe pounding on the walls with her fists. The tube shook alarmingly. He placed a steadying hand against it. 'Stay still! You might knock it over and hurt yourself. Look, I'm going to have to go get help. I can't do this alone.'

'Hurry up,' she begged, a note of panic entering her voice. 'It's dark in here.'

'I'll get someone. I won't be long. Try to stay calm. Sit down and … uh … meditate.'

'Do *what*?' At least her scornful tone showed that she wasn't losing it completely.

'Sit still and wait!' Tim turned to Theseus and gripped his arm. 'Do you think Socrates might know how to solve it? He's smart.'

But the hero shook his head. 'Not that kind of smart. Socrates would talk to the tube until it bursts open from pure frustration.' He shook Tim's hand off. 'Careful, I've just moisturised.'

'There must be someone.'

Tim didn't want to call Hercules – mainly because that's what Hera had told him to do. Tim knew the not-too-bright hero would have trouble solving the puzzle. A code "as easy as pie"? Tim didn't believe it. This had to be a trap — a way to lure Hercules and capture him while he was busy thinking. Why else would Hera create a code? If all she wanted to do was imprison Zoe, she wouldn't have given them a way out.

Tim refused to play into the goddess' hands. No. He would solve this without Hercules' help.

'How about Pythagoras? Yeah! Great idea.' Theseus tapped the side of his forehead and beamed. 'See I'm not just beautiful: I have brains, too. Pythagoras is the man we need.'

Tim had heard of the ancient mathematician. Who hadn't? The Pythagorean theorem was one of the things Tim had struggled with in his test. What was it again? *A* squared plus *B* squared equalled, err … the sum of the square of the hypotenuse … oh gosh. He felt a sweat break out on his brow. It was something to do with right-angled triangles, he knew that much.

But Theseus was right. A mathematician would be the perfect person to crack a combination lock. 'Do you know where we can find him?' Tim asked eagerly.

'Sure do. I saw him not long ago. This way!'

Tim called out to Zoe that they'd be back soon. With a last worried glance at Hera's temple and the puzzle prison, he scurried after the hero.

■　■　■

They found the mathematician striding through a nearby field, his cloak fluttering in the breeze. His hair and beard were a deep dark red and he had penetrating grey eyes. With his wide domed forehead, Pythagoras did indeed look very intelligent. Tim explained their problem and the mathematician agreed to help.

It felt strange to be talking to the inventor of a formula that every child in the world had to learn. Larry's refusal to help him with maths didn't matter anymore, Tim realised. He could go straight to the source!

'Do you mind quickly explaining your theorem?' Tim panted as they bustled back to Zoe. 'I know you're already doing us a big favour, but seeing as you're here anyway–'

'You mean my views on the transmigration of the soul?' The man's

eyes gleamed with a strange intensity.

'Trans-my-what?' Was that some maths term that Tim had never heard of before?

'My followers and I believe that when a person dies, their soul may be reborn inside an animal's body.'

'You what?' This was a side of Pythagoras that Tim hadn't known about.

'That's why we shouldn't eat animals,' the mathematician continued, slowing his pace. 'There might be a human soul inside. You don't devour flesh, I trust?'

'Err…' Tim decided not to mention the roast beef that Mum had cooked for dinner.

'I can't help you if you've polluted your body and spirit by eating meat.'

'Please, we need you! I promise I'll never eat another burger again!' At that moment, Tim really meant it.

He gazed at the mathematician imploringly. Not looking where he was going, Tim accidentally trod on the tail of a small brown dog that had been sleeping on the path. It bounced up with a yelp.

'Hey, that sounded like Meliton!' Pythagoras scurried over and squatted next to the little dog. 'My dear dead friend Meliton. Is that you? I'd know your voice anywhere.'

Tim stared at Pythagoras in dismay. Was this man really a brilliant mathematician? Surely someone so smart couldn't be so … odd!

'Do you live inside a dog now? Did
the careless boy hurt you?' Pythagoras
hugged the dog, who didn't look too
pleased about it. Wriggling out of the
man's grasp, it cocked its leg against a

rock. It let out a stream of steaming urine and then stalked haughtily away.

'That's Meliton all right.' Pythagoras nodded with satisfaction. 'That's exactly what he used to do upon waking.' He pulled himself to his feet and turned to Tim. 'You should watch where you step,' he said coldly.

'I'm sorry. I didn't see him! I'll be more careful.'

Pythagoras grunted. 'Humph. You eat meat, you walk all over my friends. Why should I help you? Maybe I should turn around and go home.'

Tim felt a sense of hopelessness wash over him. Could Pythagoras really rescue Zoe, or was this all a waste of time? It was hard to believe that the bizarre man standing next to him was a genius. Still, Tim didn't have many other options.

'Don't leave! It's my friend you're helping, not me.'

The mathematician didn't look convinced. 'Does she eat meat?'

'I've never seen her eat it,' Tim answered truthfully. 'Please come. I promise I won't step on your friends again.'

'Well, I don't know …' Pythagoras pulled a face and turned away. Something he saw, however, made him suddenly go rigid. 'Ach, no!'

'What's wrong?' Tim asked, following his gaze. There was nothing out of the ordinary – at least, nothing that Tim could see.

Pythagoras was glaring at a vegetable patch at the side of the road. Rows of glossy green plants wound their way up evenly spaced wooden stakes. Tim could see long, plump pods dangling off the stalks, like icicles on a Christmas tree.

Beans.

Tim wasn't particularly fond of beans, but didn't see why they should upset the mathematician so much.

'What's wrong with—' he started to say.

'I keep telling people! Never eat beans!' Pythagoras held up his hands in a warding-off gesture, making a triangle with his thumbs and index fingers. It was like watching someone make a crucifix shape to scare off a vampire.

'How come? I know they're yuck but …'

'They make you break wind! That's the problem.' Pythagoras spoke so vehemently, a fine spray of spit flew from his mouth.

Tim shrugged. Sitting next to Leo in class had made him all too familiar with other people's farts. Gross, but not worth getting so worked up about.

'When you break wind, you lose part of your soul!' The mathematician wrung his hands in despair. 'I keep telling people that, but do they listen? We must destroy the crop before it's too late.' His cloak billowing behind him, Pythagoras left the path and strode towards the vegetable patch.

Was this guy for real?

'Not now,' Tim squawked. 'My friend's

trapped–' But then he saw something that made *him* stop and stare in horror.

A flock of peacocks suddenly flew towards them and landed among the crop rows. They fell on the beans hungrily, snapping at the pods with their sharp beaks. Were they Hera's peacocks, or ordinary birds that were simply looking for lunch? Surely flocks of wild peacocks didn't exist in Greece? They had to be Hera's! Maybe the goddess had realised that Tim had disobeyed her instructions and sent her birds out to look for him.

They had to leave before the birds spotted him and started calling their mistress.

'Hey! Get out of there.' Pythagoras flapped his hands at the birds.

'We have to go.' Tim tugged at the man's cloak.

Pythagoras swung around to face him. 'I will only help you if you stop the birds. There might be human souls inside them. You know what'll happen if the birds eat the beans? They'll break wind!'

Tim realised there was no point in arguing with the mathematician. If Tim wanted Pythagoras' help, he had to do it his way – even at the risk of alerting Hera. Tim made shooing gestures with his hands, but the big blue birds ignored him and kept eating.

'Theseus, help us,' he called over.

The hero had been standing around looking bored. On hearing his name, he adopted a heroic pose before springing into action. 'Go away, birdies. Shoo.'

Tim thought he could hear Hera's laughter drift by, but it might have been the wind.

'This is too awful,' the mathematician wailed.

Tim watched Theseus' leather pouch jiggle as he waved his arms at the birds.

It gave him an idea. Squinting against the bright sunlight, he asked to borrow the hero's mirror, which was kept in the pouch.

'Not now. Fix your hair later, after we've triumphed. Really! You don't know much about being a hero.' Theseus rolled his eyes.

'That's not what I mean. It's to stop the birds.'

'They're not gorgons, you know. I don't think a mirror's going to help.'

Tim didn't want to waste time with explanations. 'Just ... give it to me, please.' Tim held out his hand and the hero reluctantly dug the mirror out of the pouch.

'Careful not to scratch it,' Theseus

warned, handing it over.

Tim stepped back. He glanced from the birds to the sky. It was all about getting the angle right. If he held the mirror just so … up a bit … to the left … down … A stream of bright sunlight bounced off the mirror's shiny surface. With a deft flick of the wrist, Tim beamed it straight into the birds' eyes.

At first it didn't seem to be working, but then Tim noticed some of the birds blinking. They closed their eyes and twitched their heads in irritation. After a while they started to

turn away. It was working! Keeping his hands steady, Tim refocused the beam. More birds turned away. It occurred to him that getting the angle right required some pretty complex calculations. And he was doing it! Tim smiled. Before too long, the whole flock stopped eating and turned tail, clearly annoyed by the beams of light.

'There we are!' said Tim. 'Done. Let's go rescue Zoe.' He handed the mirror back to Theseus, who brushed off a speck of dust before putting it carefully away.

Pythagoras frowned. 'We have to destroy the crop, before anything else tries to eat the beans.'

'We can't waste any more time,' Tim said, his voice rising with frustration. 'We have to help my friend now.'

Something, perhaps the sound of Tim's voice, made the birds look up. They focused their beady eyes on him, paused as if thinking, and then started to squawk and flap their wings. They must be calling Hera!

'Run!' Tim shouted.

'Hurry up!' Tim grabbed Pythagoras by the arm and dragged him back onto the path. The mathematician protested but clamped his mouth shut when Theseus threatened to feed him a bean.

'We can deal with the crop later,' Tim promised. 'Once Zoe is free.'

Luckily, they managed to leave the birds behind them before Hera could turn up. Tim looked around nervously as they neared her temple. There was no sign of her. Maybe she was at the vegetable patch, looking for Tim and his friends. It wouldn't take her long to realise they'd left – and she'd easily guess where they'd gone.

Tim walked up to the puzzle prison and laid his palms against it. 'This is it,' he said, fighting down a sense of urgency. Feeling rushed was no way to approach a puzzle: it only made you take longer. 'Zoe, are you okay in there?'

'You took your time!' she fumed. 'Get on with it!'

Tim patted the puzzle reassuringly then pulled away. 'Any ideas?' he asked Pythagoras hopefully.

'Hmm.' The mathematician stroked his chin and circled around the tube. 'The letters are all mixed up, not in alphabetical order. I wonder if that means anything?'

Tim blinked. How would he know?

'This is very tricky. Did the goddess give you any clues?' Pythagoras asked.

'No. Hang on. Maybe. Theseus, what did she say about pies?'

The hero shrugged. 'I never eat pies. They're bad for the figure.' He started examining his mirror, running his finger over the surface and checking for scratches.

'Oh, I remember. Hera said the code was as "easy as pie".' Tim looked at the mathematician hopefully. 'Does that mean anything to you?'

'Pie?' Pythagoras raised his eyebrows. 'As in Pie-thagoras? She might have been referring to me! Maybe the code is something to do with my theory as to the transmigration of souls.'

'Mmmaybe …' It didn't sound likely.

'Hold on! I get it! *Pi*!' Pythagoras slapped himself on his broad forehead. 'Of course. The mathematical symbol π. The

ratio of the circumference of a circle to its diameter.'

'Okay.' Tim had no idea what Pythagoras was talking about, but it sounded promising.

'Let me see … if you divide the two … that makes it approximately … hmm …' Pythagoras continued to mumble as he shifted the bands around, one after the other, snapping them deftly into place.

Tim looked on expectantly, his hopes rising. The mathematician certainly seemed to know what he was doing! Finally, Pythagoras stopped. He wiped a hand across his brow.

Tim watched and waited. 'What's next?' he said after a few moments had passed.

'That's it.'

'But – nothing's happening!'

'I can't help that. I've never trusted irrational numbers, and Pi is irrational.'

'I … I …' Tim didn't know what to say to that.

'Get. Me. Out.' Clearly out of patience, Zoe started thudding on the walls again.

'Maybe we should try Socrates after all,' Theseus said, playing with his mirror. 'I know I said he's the wrong sort of smart, but' – the hero shrugged – 'this isn't getting us far. Besides, I fancy a trip to the agora. You never know who you might meet there.'

Tim couldn't come up with a better plan.

'Can you keep trying, please?' he said to Pythagoras, flashing a weak smile. 'We'll be right back.'

. . .

The journey to the agora didn't take long. Theseus seemed quite keen to reach the public space. 'If I see anyone interesting, I'm leaving,' the hero warned Tim, rubbing his hands together. 'My fans will want to know all about this latest adventure.'

Tim didn't think there'd be much to tell, but he didn't mind if Theseus left. The journey seemed simple enough and he wasn't much help anyway. 'All right.'

'That's Socrates.' Theseus nodded. 'The

one with the big flat nose.'

Tim followed the hero's gaze. Strolling around the agora was an old man with receding grey hair and a long curly beard. A grubby white sheet was wrapped around his waist, and another sheet was slung over one shoulder. Tim had expected that Socrates would have a big retinue of followers, but – for the moment at least – he was on his own.

'Oh good.' Tim turned to thank Theseus, but the hero had already left. Tim saw him swaggering towards a group of young women, who giggled at his approach.

Tim squared his shoulders and went up to the old man. 'Hello. Are you Socrates?'

The old man stared at Tim as if he had just asked an intriguing question. 'I might be. Or I might not. Who is to say?'

Tim thought that perhaps he had the wrong person, but then it hit him: Socrates was famous for challenging everything. Tim still had no idea how to answer such a question though.

'I'm looking for the wise philosopher,' he said haltingly.

The old man raised an index finger into the air. 'Ah, but what is wisdom? If there is one thing that I know, it is that I know nothing.'

Tim blinked. 'Okay. I just—'

'Actually,' said Socrates, stroking his beard and looking thoughtful. 'That's a good line. I must be wise indeed if I can come up with that! Someone should write that down.'

'I'll write it down for you, if you like,' Tim promised, 'if you'll agree to help me. A friend of mine is trapped in a puzzle prison. Only someone as clever as you can get her out. Will you help?'

'I have no objection to helping.' Socrates paused. 'Unless *you* can think of an objection …'

Tim shook his head. 'Please. It's important.'

'Then I shall help.'

The old man walked very slowly and Tim had to force himself to be patient. Maybe he was worrying for nothing. Maybe Pythagoras had managed to release Zoe after all. The philosopher seemed to be in the mood to talk, so Tim decided he might as well ask the question he'd had in mind all along – the reason he'd come back to Ancient Greece in the first place.

'I was wondering,' Tim began, 'how do you know if someone will be a good father?'

Socrates tapped his fingertips together. 'Well, my boy, that depends on what you mean by "good".'

'Well, *good*. You know. Not bad.' Tim thought about it. 'Kind.'

'Ah, but what do you mean by "kind"?'

Tim was stumped. Maybe he needed to explain himself more clearly. 'My mother has a suitor, and I don't know whether or not he'll be a good stepfather. If they get married, that is. Which they might not.' He could feel himself getting more tongue-tied as the philosopher smiled down at him, his face serene and untroubled.

'Do you think it's up to you whether they marry or not?' Socrates asked.

'No. Yes. I don't know.' Feeling uncomfortable, Tim dropped his gaze. He suddenly found that he didn't want to talk about it anymore. 'Maybe you can just help me get my friend out,' he muttered.

'Well, that depends on what you mean by "friend".'

'Oh gosh.' Tim looked at the philosopher, who was nodding importantly and looking pleased with himself.

Tim felt his spirits sink.

When they returned to the puzzle prison, Tim saw that nothing had changed. Pythagoras was scratching his head and twisting bands, and Zoe was still locked up.

'I've brought help.' Tim turned to the philosopher. 'My friend's trapped in there. Can you solve the code and let her out?'

Socrates smiled and shook his head sadly, as if he were facing a particularly dim pupil. 'There are no traps, except for those found within the mind.'

Tim did a swift double take. What was he on about? 'But – but my friend's inside that thing. She wants to get out.'

'Why does she want to get out?' Arms folded, Socrates leant against the giant cylinder. 'Why is it bad to be imprisoned? What does it mean for something to be bad? And who decides anyway – is it the gods or is it man?'

'No – it's a girl,' came Zoe's flustered voice. 'Me! And I say get me out.'

'Do you mind?' Pythagoras said to Socrates, his voice tetchy. 'I'm trying to solve this puzzle, and I can't do that while you're leaning all over it.'

Socrates smiled indulgently but didn't budge. 'Tell me, friend, why are you trying to solve the puzzle?'

'Because I was asked to help, of course.'

'Why?'

'Why was I asked?' Pythagoras looked flustered. 'B-because I'm smart, I guess.'

'What makes you smarter than anyone else?'

The mathematician frowned. 'I don't know.' He stopped to think about it. 'Maybe it's because I don't eat beans.'

Socrates nodded knowingly. 'So if everyone stopped eating beans, they would all be as clever as you.'

'Yes– No. I don't think so. I must have been born smart.'

'Why you, and not someone else?'

'I suppose … I was lucky?' The mathematician's voice trailed away uncertainly.

'And why should you be lucky, rather than someone else? What makes you more worthy than any other man?'

'Because … I, uh, erm … Ach, I don't need to justify myself to you.' Pythagoras

wrapped his cloak tightly around his body.
'I've had enough of this. I'm going back
to the vegetable patch to destroy those
beans.' Eyes blazing, he strode off without
a backwards glance.

'Wait for me,' Socrates called after him.
'I want to teach you more about your own
ignorance. Slow down!'

Without saying goodbye to Tim, the
philosopher turned and started hobbling
after Pythagoras.

Tim didn't try to call them back. There
was no point. They weren't going to solve
the puzzle anyway: Pythagoras was over-
complicating things and Socrates wouldn't
even try. There was only one other person
that Tim knew who was a maths whizz.

Larry.

Tim would have to go home and ask for his help. This time, he wouldn't take no for an answer.

• • •

Tim retrieved the vase and landed back in his bedroom. Voices drifted up the staircase. Worried voices, talking in a low murmur. Tim put the vase down and nudged it against the wall with his foot.

Mum burst into his room. 'Tim, are you all right? We didn't mean to …'

Larry held up his hand. 'I'll handle this, Penny. Don't you worry.'

Handle what? Tim looked from one adult to the other. His mother looked on the verge of tears. Larry looked sheepish. What was going on? And then Tim remembered. Just before he'd gone to Greece, his mother and Larry had been arguing over Larry's refusal to help Tim with maths. All the worry about Zoe had pushed it out of his mind.

'Listen, mate,' Larry said, looking Tim in the eye. 'You and I need to have a little talk. Man to man.'

Tim nodded solemnly. He needed Larry to tell him how to solve the puzzle.

'I agree.'

'You do?' Mum's eyebrows shot up in surprise. 'All right. I'll go clear up.'

Mum lingered at the door, a worried look on her face. She left after an encouraging nod from her boyfriend.

'Have a seat.' Larry gestured towards the bed and Tim perched on the edge. The teacher dragged the chair out from under Tim's desk and sat down, folding his long legs. 'We have to work out how we'll get

along, you and I.'

'Yeah, sure. Do you know how to solve combination locks?'

'Now hear me out,' Larry said, his brow furrowing. 'I'm trying to apologise. I was wrong to say I wouldn't help you.' The teacher ran a hand through his hair. 'I want to do the right thing by you, but – to be honest, I don't know what that is. I've never been in this situation before. Do you get what I'm saying?'

Tim jiggled impatiently.

'So you have to tell me if I upset you, and I'll try to fix it,' Larry continued slowly. 'Is that okay, Tim? Tim? Are you listening to me?'

'Yes! Yes, I am. It's just … I've got a

problem.' The teacher frowned. 'Not to do with you,' Tim added. 'But I need your help.'

Larry leaned back in his chair. 'All right. Tell me.'

Now that it came down to it, Tim wasn't sure he was doing the right thing. He looked the teacher in the eye. Larry returned his gaze steadily. Could Tim trust him?

The way he saw it, there were two possible outcomes. One, Larry would believe him. He'd tell him how to solve the puzzle and Tim would free Zoe. Two, Larry wouldn't believe him and he'd walk away. The puzzle would remain unsolved and Zoe would stay trapped.

'Come on, mate,' Larry urged. 'You can trust me.'

'I don't know where to start.'

'How about you start at the beginning?'

So Tim did. It took a long time to explain everything to Larry. When he'd finished, Tim glanced anxiously at the teacher. Did he believe him? Would he help?

'So your friend's trapped and you want me to tell you how to get her out?' Larry hadn't interrupted Tim and he now spoke for the first time.

'That's right! Then I can go back and save her.'

Larry looked into Tim's eyes, long and hard. 'Is that the vase?' Without breaking eye contact, Larry pointed to where it rested against the wall. When Tim nodded, Larry stood up.

Tim stood up too. The teacher looked serious, as though he were about to make an important announcement at school assembly.

'RIGHT.
TAKE ME
TO HER.'

'What?' Tim squawked. 'I can't take you to Ancient Greece!'

'Why not?' Larry's voice was steady. 'I can't teach you to solve a puzzle I haven't seen. Take me with you. I'll get your friend out.'

'But – but …' This was an outcome that Tim hadn't predicted. What should he do?

'Never keep a girl waiting. Always remember that!' Larry picked up the vase as if the matter were settled. 'We grab the handles, right? And then I say ...'

'Hold on. Wait for me!' Tim placed his hands over the teacher's larger ones. 'Oh vase, take us back to Hera's temple.'

Larry was surprisingly quiet as they flew through the air. Tim expected him to shout or speak or at least gasp. As soon as they landed, the teacher calmly took control.

'Right. Where's your friend?' He gazed around the ancient landscape as if he were surveying something as ordinary as the school playground. His Australian accent sounded oddly out of place among the statues, shrines and colonnades.

'Tim! Is that you?' Zoe's frantic voice

sounded muffled. 'I'm still here!'

'Don't you worry,' Larry said. 'We'll have you out in a jiffy. Now let me think. What did you say the clue was? As easy as pie?' Rubbing his chin, Larry walked around the giant tube.

'I thought the letters might spell out a password, but Pythagoras was going on about maths and circles and stuff. I don't know why, though. These are letters, not numbers.'

'That's because the Ancient Greeks didn't have numbers like ours. Even Roman numerals hadn't been invented yet.' Larry shrugged. 'The Greeks used letters to stand for numbers.'

Tim shuddered. As if maths weren't

complicated enough.

'I thought "pie" might mean the number, but you said Pythagoras tried that already.'

'That's right.'

Larry tilted his head left and right. 'The letters aren't in alphabetical order. They're scattered randomly around the bands. I wonder why? There must be a reason. Hmm, pie …'

Tim held his breath and clenched his fists as the teacher started to rotate the bands.

Gaining confidence, Larry moved around nimbly, twisting and tugging and pushing. His movements were swift and sure. Before long, Tim heard a loud click. The bands were aligned so that one symbol – π – was repeated all the way down.

'As easy as the Greek letter π,' Larry explained with a grin.

It really wasn't that hard, Tim realised. He should have worked it out!

There was a loud shuddering noise. The bands of the puzzle flew apart and vanished in a dramatic puff of smoke. When it cleared, Zoe stood in its place, stunned. Her hair was in wild disarray and she blinked against the bright sunlight. As soon as she spotted Tim, she threw her arms around him.

'Thank you,' she sobbed. 'It was awful in there! Cramped. Dark. I

thought I'd never get out!'

Feeling awkward, Tim patted her on the back. 'That's okay.' He pulled away. 'This is Mr … err … Larry. My mum's boyfriend. He's the one who got you out.'

'Oh.' Zoe spun around to face the teacher. She studied him for a moment, then her face broke into a smile. 'Tim's been worried about you. He doesn't know if you'll be a good stepfather or not. I think you will be.'

'Is that so?' Larry stood, hands on hips, grinning.

Groaning, Tim wished the ground would open up and swallow him. Trust Zoe to spit it out! Like her father, she had no tact.

'What's going on here?' A deep voice

boomed and the ground shook.

It was as if Tim had conjured the hero up by thinking of him. Tim looked up and saw Hercules striding angrily towards them. His wife Agatha was with him. Her face lit up on seeing Zoe and she ran to embrace her. Zoe fell into her arms and they hugged each other tearfully.

'Tim Baker, have you endangered my daughter yet again?' Hercules thundered. 'Come and stand before me.'

Tim obeyed. 'I'm sorry,' he mumbled.

'G'day.' Larry stepped in front of him smoothly and held out his hand for the hero to shake. 'You must be Hercules. I'm Larry.'

Hercules stared at the extended hand

with bulging eyes. 'What is this? Are you challenging me to an arm wrestle? I accept your challenge.'

The hero cracked his knuckles.

'No! It's a greeting.' Tim poked his head out from behind the teacher then slunk back again when Hercules glared at him.

'Tim didn't put your daughter in harm's way,' Larry said, dropping his hand to his side. 'He rescued her. He was very brave. You should be proud of him.'

'Rescued?' The scowl left Hercules' face and he looked uncertain. 'But ... the GGG said he stood and watched while Zoe became trapped. I came here to smash the trap open with my bare hands and get her out!'

'But Tim beat you to it,' Larry said. 'If it weren't for him she'd still be stuck. I hope you realise it took courage for him to confide in me and ask for my help. I might not have trusted him. I might have let him down, like others have done today.'

'I hope you are not referring to me!' Hercules said, his eyebrows meeting in the middle. 'I have never let my friend down.'

'Of course not. But Tim didn't want to worry you. He wanted to solve the problem himself.' Larry stepped beside Tim and put a hand on his shoulder. 'You should be thanking him for saving your daughter.'

'Oh. I see. Well then, thank you, Tim Baker,' the hero said gruffly. He looked solemn for a moment, then picked Tim up in a huge embrace that left him gasping for air.

'You're welcome,' Tim managed to squeak.

'Who did you say you were?' Hercules said after he put Tim down. He examined the teacher carefully. 'You are from the future. I can tell by your strange clothes.'

'This is my mother's boyfriend.'

'Her suitor?' Hercules walked all the way around Larry, looking him up and down. 'You seem a rather puny specimen. Do you consider yourself to be a worthy stepfather for my friend?'

Oh no. Tim felt like sinking into the ground again. What was it with Hercules and Zoe? Now Mr Green would know how worried he'd been.

'I hope so … one day.' Larry smiled and ruffled Tim's hair. 'We're not quite at that stage yet. Let's just be mates for now, okay?'

Relieved, Tim was about to reply when Hercules interrupted. 'Not so fast. First, I must test you. I must see for myself whether you are worthy.'

'That's not necess–' Tim started to say.

'I will put you through a series of labours,' the hero announced. 'They will test all the elements that make up a man: strength, courage and strength. Do you accept? Or do you fear failure?'

'Don't do it!' Tim squawked. He tugged Larry's wrist. 'Let's go home now. You don't need to prove anything.'

But Larry was already taking off his jacket. Dropping it on the ground, he looked Hercules in the eye.

'Ready when you are, mate.'

11

'Have you heard of the Horses of Diomedes?' Hercules asked. He rubbed his hands together and his black eyes glittered.

'Can't say that I have.' The teacher looked remarkably calm.

'I speak of one of my twelve labours. Not the hardest – we shall begin with something simple. See, Tim Baker, I am being kind to the puny little man.'

Larry wasn't at all puny, Tim thought. Not compared to other men. But compared to Hercules, even an elephant looked frail.

'Tell me more,' Larry said calmly.

'Diomedes was a wicked king of a barbarous people,' Hercules said. 'He fed his horses with human flesh, thus turning them into man-eaters.'

Tim winced. He was glad Pythagoras wasn't around to hear that. It would have deeply upset the vegetarian mathematician.

'I was given the task of capturing these vile beasts,' Hercules said, warming to his story. 'It would have been simple but for one thing: I had to bring them back alive. I overpowered them and tied them to a chariot. All the while they kept trying to bite chunks out of me. It was not pleasant.'

Tim could imagine. He wasn't sure where this was going, but he had the uncomfortable feeling that he was about to find out.

'I managed to tame them and put them to useful work on a farm. But – unfortunately – some of them have gone wild again.'

Larry nodded. 'I hear you, mate. I've had a few boys at school go feral on me, too.'

'They are not boys, they are man-eaters!' Hercules slapped his hand against his palm. 'There is no comparison. Boys do not bite your legs off and chew them up.'

'We know one who might try, don't we, Tim?' Larry winked.

Tim guessed he was referring to Leo,

and suppressed a giggle.

'This is no time for laughter,' the hero reprimanded them. 'Two of these horses have escaped. Even as we speak they roam the outskirts of town, looking for travellers to eat. An alert went out on the GGG. I think this is the perfect chance for your mother's suitor to prove himself.'

'He can't capture wild horses,' Tim said, clutching at Larry's sleeve.

'He only needs to capture one,' said Hercules. 'I shall catch the other myself. Or is Larry Mr Green not up to the challenge?'

Tim looked at Larry expectantly. Surely he would refuse. He wasn't a fighter; he was a teacher. He would tell Tim to pick up the vase and take them home to safety. Tim waited.

'You're on,' Larry told the hero. 'Let's go.'

Zoe cheered. Tim stuttered out an objection but Larry merely winked at him. Was the man insane? Great. That's all Tim needed: a crazy future stepfather! Or even worse, a seriously maimed crazy future stepfather. Hercules led the way. As he walked, he talked. About his twelve labours. About his many heroic deeds … Larry seemed to be enjoying the tales. He nodded and grunted in all the right places.

Tim, Zoe and Agatha lagged behind the two men, who walked with energy and enthusiasm. After passing a final scattering of houses, they reached the outskirts of town. Apart from a dense olive grove, there was nothing much to see. No man-eating horses. No half-chewed travellers. Tim let out a breath. Maybe the horses wouldn't show up. Maybe they'd been caught already. Maybe …

Maybe it was a trap! For the first time, it occurred to Tim to wonder who had actually put out the GGG alert. What if it were Hera? What if the whole thing was a ploy to lure them to the olive grove? Tim looked around anxiously and kept his ears strained for the sound of calling peacocks.

Suddenly a cloud of dust appeared over the horizon. Tim shielded his eyes and squinted into the distance. Was it Hera's birds? The man-eating horses? Or it might be something less dangerous like … er … a tornado. But tornadoes don't have pounding hooves. They don't snicker and neigh. Tim heard the horses before he saw them. It didn't take long for them to emerge from the choking dust cloud. Tails swishing, feet flying, manes whipping in the wind. The horses rolled their eyes and bared their teeth, which were sharp and pointed like wolves' fangs. As they snorted, clouds of steam rose from their nostrils.

'Girls, Tim, get back!' Hercules shouted. 'I'll take the big one – it's closer. You get the other.' He looked at Larry,

who flinched and then shook himself.

Before Tim could object, Hercules raced forward. He flung himself at the first horse's flank. 'Think you're stronger than me?' he snarled, rolling the animal onto its back. 'I caught you once, I'll catch you again!'

Narrowing its eyes, the second horse galloped towards Larry. The teacher didn't hurl himself at it, however. Instead, he shouted something that Tim couldn't hear, then dashed into the nearby olive grove. Stunned, Tim stood rooted to the spot. Was the teacher running away? Confronted with danger, he chose to abandon everyone and flee. Pausing only to scoop something off the ground, Larry clambered up an olive tree, out of reach of the horse's sharp teeth. Tim's suspicions were confirmed. Larry had left them behind!

How could he? Mr Green had acted so calm and in control.

That's what it was, Tim realised, his heart pounding. An act. The teacher didn't care about anyone but himself. No way did he want this man to be his stepfather.

'Tim!' Zoe shrieked.

Changing direction, the second horse abandoned its pursuit of the teacher. Instead, shaking its head and flaring its nostrils, the great beast headed straight towards Tim, Zoe and Agatha.

'Quick, the trees!' Tim grabbed Zoe and Agatha's hands and dragged them into the same olive grove that Larry had fled into. 'Climb,' he urged them.

Zoe didn't take long to catch on. Hand over hand, she scrambled up the nearest silvery trunk. She did it so quickly and easily, that Tim guessed she'd had lots of practice. Agatha, however, stood frozen. Her back pressed against the tree, she stared at

the fast-approaching
horse, her eyes wide with
fear. Tim suspected that the
elegant woman had never
climbed a tree before.

'Climb up, quickly.
You can do it!' he shouted.
'I'll give you a leg up.' Trying
to suppress a violent tremble,
Tim linked his hands together.
He lowered them near the
ground, providing the older
woman with a foothold.
Using all his strength, he
hoisted her up as hard as
he could. Agatha's hands
flailed and she gasped. It

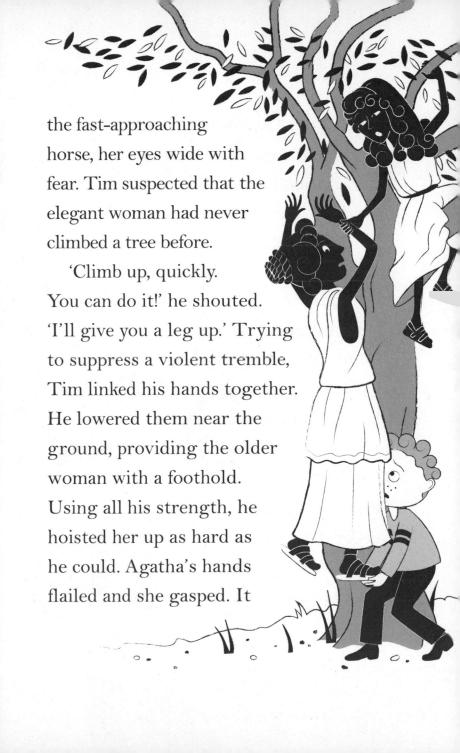

looked like she was about to topple over backwards.

'Ma!' Zoe called. Leaning down from her high perch, the girl caught her mother's arms and steadied her. With a final glance over her shoulder, Agatha gained her balance and started to climb.

Now that Agatha and Zoe were safe, Tim looked around. There wasn't enough room in the tree for the three of them, so Tim climbed another. There wasn't

time to pick and choose, however, as the horse had started to crash its way into the olive grove. Tim scrambled upwards. It was only once he settled on a branch that he realised his tree was right next to Larry's. The teacher was close enough to touch.

'Good on you, mate,' Larry said, flashing a lopsided grin. 'I wasn't sure if you'd heard me, but I knew you'd see the girls safe.'

Tim pressed his lips together

and turned his face away. He refused to speak to him. He wouldn't look at him either. What was the point?

A large *crack* made Tim twist back around.

Larry had broken a small branch off the tree. It was bent at a right angle, like a triangle with one side missing. 'This'll do,' he said. The teacher reached into his shirt pocket and pulled out a long, sharp-edged stone. It looked like a knife blade. Tim guessed it was the object Larry had picked off the ground before climbing the tree. What was he doing? 'This is a little trick I learnt in the outback,' Larry said, rapidly carving the bent olive branch. 'I spent my first year of teaching in the bush. I made friends with some of the Aboriginal fellas and they showed me how to do this.' Big curls of wood peeled off the branch and fell to the ground. 'Never had to work so fast before, but no worries. I can do it.'

The horse was directly beneath them. Tim felt his tree shudder as the mighty beast rammed the trunk with its powerful head. He could feel the heat rising off the sweating body. He could hear its rasping breath. Shuddering, Tim gripped the branch tighter.

Larry kept carving as the tree shook. The wood was rapidly taking on a smooth

curved shape, the top surface rounded like an aeroplane's wings. 'This shape's called a parabola, by the way,' he said. 'You'll study them in maths one day. I'll explain it when you do. But for now–' Larry let the rock fall to the ground. He held the wooden object by one edge and balanced it in his outstretched hand. 'For now … how do you like my boomerang?'

Before Tim could reply, the teacher took a deep breath. 'Wish me luck, mate.'

Larry slithered to the ground, darted around the horse and ran to the edge of the grove. 'Come on, you old ratbag!' he called to the enraged animal. 'What are you waiting for?' He took off at high speed into the clearing.

The horse abandoned Tim's tree and galloped after Larry. Eyes bulging, Tim held on tight and watched. As soon as the horse broke into the clearing, the teacher pulled back his arm and leant into the breeze. With a flick of the wrist, he let the boomerang fly. It whirred as it traced a wide, curved shape.

The horse didn't see it coming. One second the man-eater was rearing up on its hind legs, nostrils flaring, teeth bared. The next second there was a loud *thunk!* and the horse toppled over, like a tree that had been felled. Tim saw Hercules striding towards them and he made his way down the tree, knowing that it was finally safe. Zoe and Agatha also came down, the latter looking relieved to be on solid ground again. Soon they were standing together in front of the fallen horse.

'I'll just whip this round before it wakes up,' Larry said, taking off his belt. He twisted it around the horse's nose and mouth, making a crude muzzle. He fastened the buckle and pulled the belt tight.

Hercules grunted encouragements as he watched Larry work. Not far away, the first horse was similarly muzzled. It was resting on its knees, gazing around dazedly as if wondering what had happened. All the fight had gone out of the animal as it peered at them through lowered lids.

'Excellent.' Hercules beamed his approval. 'These two will be pulling a chariot again in no time. When they've recovered, I'll take them back where they came from. And now' – he rubbed his hands together – 'time for another challenge!'

'I think one will do.' Agatha laid a restraining hand on her husband's arm. She had recovered her composure very quickly. 'This man has proved himself already. He has shown he has strength, courage and–'

'Strength,' Hercules finished.

'Surely that's enough to be getting on with,' Agatha said, tilting her head and smiling at Tim.

'I agree,' Tim said, before Hercules could come up with an objection. He felt bad about doubting Larry. But how was he to know what the teacher was planning? He couldn't hear what he'd said!

Zoe scooped up the carved object that Larry had hurled at the horse. Turning it over in her hands, she said, 'What's this?'

'It's a boomerang,' Larry said, shading his eyes from the sun. 'They're well known where I come from. If you throw one properly, it traces a circle and comes back.'

'Is that so?' a soft voice hissed. 'My my, aren't you clever?' It came from the direction of the olive grove.

Tim felt his blood run cold. He knew that voice! Emerging from the dappled shade of the trees was a slim figure in an ivory gown. A wispy veil trailed from her delicate crown. The evil goddess locked her pale blue eyes with Larry's deep green ones as she sashayed towards them.

13

Hera smiled broadly at Larry as she approached. It didn't make Tim feel any better. It was a dangerous smile – a predator's smile. He glanced sideways at Larry to see whether he had been taken in. The teacher wasn't smiling back, Tim saw to his relief. Instead he had a calm, reflective look on his face.

'Never smile at a crocodile,' Larry murmured.

Tim nodded.

'What are you doing here?' Zoe asked, bristling at the goddess. Being trapped in a puzzle prison and then chased up a tree by a man-eating horse seemed to have made her more tetchy than usual.

'I'm returning your amphora,' Hera said, her eyes wide and innocent. 'You left it near my temple, after you

finished playing with my little puzzle. Very careless.' She shook her head in sorrow. 'You wouldn't want it to get into the wrong hands.'

Tim face-palmed. With all the worry and excitement, they had forgotten to take the vase! Hera was right. He was getting careless.

'Where is it? What have you done with it? I'll smash it before you can use it to catch my dad,' Zoe said. She raised the boomerang threateningly, but Hercules stood in front of her and glared at Hera.

'Don't ever come near my daughter again,' he growled.

'Like I said, I'm returning the amphora,' Hera said, pointing.

Tim followed the goddess' outstretched finger. There, nestling under a tree, was the magic vase! Hera wasn't lying. But what was her motive? Surely she hadn't had a change of heart? In any case, he should grab it before she changed her mind. Tim turned to make a dash for it, but Larry put a restraining hand on his shoulder.

'Thank you, ma'am.' Larry nodded at Hera. 'Much appreciated. We'll be going home now, back to our own time. We don't want to keep you.'

'Oh. But I might want to keep *you*.' She looked Larry up and down approvingly.

Was the queen goddess flirting? Tim wondered in shock. *Yuck!*

'He is betrothed,' Agatha put in, her

voice severe. 'Leave mortals alone, Hera. They are not for you.'

'Silence! I always get what I want. I managed to bring you all here, did I not?' Hera gazed at the muzzled, puzzled horses. 'Who do you think turned them wild again? I sent a plague of giant horse flies to sting them relentlessly until they were driven insane and escaped their bonds.'

For the first time, Tim felt a pang of pity for the powerful beasts.

'I knew you'd come here,' the goddess continued. 'Away from the prying eyes of other do-gooder gods. So now that you're here, you can enter the vase. All of you.' She turned to Larry. 'Except, perhaps, for you. If you would like to join me?' She cocked her head to the side and left her question hanging in the air.

'Like Agatha said, I'm spoken for. Anyway, you're not my type. I prefer someone younger,' Larry said drily. 'Like, say, under 2000 years old.'

A look of fury flashed across Hera's face. 'Right! Don't say I didn't give you a chance. You shall join your friends, trapped for all eternity.'

Larry folded his arms across his chest. His lop-sided grin returned. 'I don't know whether you've noticed this, ma'am, but there's only one of you.

There are five of us.'

'Do not be so sure!' Hera drew herself to her full height. 'My petals? Come to me!'

With a golden flash, a dozen peacocks suddenly appeared. Squawking aggressively, they huddled protectively around the goddess.

'Now that I have my army, you cannot stop me! I will curse you all!' She took a deep breath and raised her arms dramatically. Tim felt his heart leap in his chest.

'Not if I curse you first,' Larry said matter-of-factly.

Hera bristled. 'Ha! It is not possible. You are mortal. I am the queen of Mount Olympus!'

'But I come from the future,' Larry said, digging his hand into his pocket. 'You have no idea what powers we mortals have developed over the last few thousand years. Powers to rival the gods!'

'You are bluffing,' Hera declared. Her chin was held high but her voice was uncertain.

'Then how do you explain this?' Larry pulled out his mobile phone. He swiped at the screen and jabbed at it rapidly, until Tim heard a familiar voice emerge from the speaker. It was Mum! Laughing and talking into the camera while Larry videoed her on his phone.

'See this woman?' Larry flashed the camera towards the goddess. 'I shrank

her and trapped her inside this little box.'
His voice grew deeper and his expression
more serious. 'I can trap you too.'

'Ha! You may be able to trap a mortal
woman – but I am a different matter.' The
defiance in Hera's voice did not match the
sudden wariness in her eyes. She took an
uncertain step backwards and clenched
her fists defensively. 'You have no power
to curse me.'

'Then listen to this.'
Larry gripped his
mobile phone with
both hands and
raised it high
above his head.
'Queen Hera,

wife of Zeus, goddess of Mount Olympus.
I hereby curse you.' Lowering his arms,
he pointed the phone directly at Hera and
fixed her with a piercing stare. 'May your
peacocks turn into emus and–'

'STOP!'

Hera shrieked. She slapped her palms
against her ears to block out the words.
'Come, my petals!' In a mist of golden

sparkles, the shaken
goddess and
her peacocks
disappeared. Tim
was relieved
to see that

in her haste, she left the vase behind. Careless, he thought, grinning.

Zoe, Hercules and Agatha shared a group hug. Tim turned to Larry, who'd stopped mid-sentence and was putting his phone away.

'What were you about to say?' Tim asked, curious.

Larry smiled sheepishly. 'It's an Australian saying. "May your chooks turn into emus and kick your dunny door down." Dunny is Aussie slang for toilet, back from when people had outdoor loos.

162

It's not really a curse, of course. It just means you wish someone bad luck.' He chuckled. 'Good, isn't it?'

Laughing, Tim agreed that it was.

It was time to make their goodbyes. Hercules told Tim he could come back any time he liked. Zoe clapped with delight and Tim sighed with relief. The hero didn't stay angry for long, thankfully. He had forgiven him for placing his daughter in danger. Maybe because Tim had worked so hard to free her.

'Next time, promise to be more careful,' Hercules said. 'Avoid that wicked Hera so that I need not rush to the rescue again. I do not wish to leave my honey cake half eaten, like I did today. I'm starving.' He patted his belly. 'And I still need to deliver those horses to their owner. It will be a long time until the next meal,' he added regretfully.

How could Tim promise to avoid Hera? She was bound to be as angry as ever. Even more so if she worked out that Larry had made a fool of her with the mobile phone trick. Tim had noticed that Hera looked very shaken when confronted with something from the future that she didn't understand. Would that make her back off? Or would it make her even more dangerous?

'We'll try,' was the best Tim could say. He would certainly aim to keep out of Hera's way – but would the angry goddess stay out of his? He doubted it.

Hercules turned to Larry. 'You have shown that you possess the three things a man needs to be a good father. Strength, courage and–'

'Strength?' Larry finished for him.

'Correct.' Hercules slapped Larry on the back and laughed. 'You have my approval, Larry Mr Green. You are good enough for my friend Tim Baker.'

'And I'm glad he has a friend like you,' Larry returned. 'Shake?' He held out his hand and the hero shook it, pumping it up and down enthusiastically.

While Larry and Hercules exchanged more compliments, Agatha pulled Tim aside and spoke in a soft voice. 'There's another quality that's just as important as strength and courage, don't you think? Maybe even more important.' She looked at him questioningly. 'Do you know what I'm talking about?'

Tim hazarded a guess. 'Intelligence?' Without Larry's quick thinking the day might have ended in disaster. Then again, Pythagoras and Socrates were

very smart, but they weren't much help.

'He certainly has that!' Agatha agreed. 'But I was thinking of something else. Something that might not have occurred to you yet ...' She hesitated.

'What?' Tim wanted to know.

'Trustworthiness,' Agatha said, her eyes solemn. 'You trusted him enough to ask for his help today. But can you trust him not to speak of this to your mother? He may feel it's his duty. He might not like to keep secrets from her. And if he does – she might not want you to return.'

Tim swallowed.

'Right then.' Larry joined Tim and dropped a hand onto his shoulder. 'Time to go. Your mum will wonder where we've gone. She'll be frantic. I'm not sure how we'll explain all this to her.'

'We don't need to!' Tim yelped, jumping. 'Didn't I tell you? The vase takes us back to a few seconds after we left. She won't even know we left.'

'Hmm. I see.' Larry rubbed his chin and looked thoughtful.

Tim examined the teacher's face anxiously. Would he want to tell Mum anyway? It was impossible to tell.

'Still, we'd better go,' Larry said. 'I'm feeling quite peckish too. I wonder what's for dessert?'

■   ■   ■

Tim felt nervous as they both gripped

the vase's handles and flew home. It deposited them in his bedroom and Tim's hands shook as he released the vase. The sound of cutlery clattering in the kitchen reminded him of what was happening when they'd left. Mum had said she'd let Tim and Larry talk, while she cleared up the dinner plates.

'What an exciting life you have!' Larry said, easing the vase onto the floor. 'It gets pretty dangerous at times, by the look of it.'

Tim shrugged. He didn't know where this was going. Was the teacher about to say he had to tell Mum?

'Thanks for trusting me and asking me to help your friend.' Larry perched on Tim's chair then added, 'And sorry again about the maths. We can go through it tonight, if you like.'

Tim had bigger things to worry about than maths. Would Larry blab his secret? Tim shook his head. 'No thanks,' he mumbled. 'I'd better go help Mum with the dishes.'

'Wait a minute, mate. Something's still wrong. I can tell. What's up?'

'Nothing.'

'Tell me.' Larry leaned forward in the chair.

'I–'

'Take a seat.' It was clear the teacher wasn't going to let Tim simply walk away.

'All right.' Tim sat on the edge of his bed and wrung his hands. 'It's just I don't know whether I can tr– that is, can I … I mean …' and then he blurted the question out all at once. 'Are you going to tell Mum?'

Larry's eyebrows shot up his forehead. 'You mean, about today? About you being a time traveller?'

Tim bit his lip and nodded.

Larry leant back and crossed his legs. He closed his eyes for so long, it looked as if he'd fallen asleep. Finally his eyes snapped open and he appeared to have come to a decision.

Tim held his breath.

'If she asks me,' Larry said, his face serious.

'And … if she doesn't?'

The teacher shrugged. 'If she doesn't, then I don't see how the subject will come up.' He grinned his lopsided grin. 'This can be our secret – for now at least. But I have to warn you. If I ever think you're in real danger, I will tell her. For your own safety.'

Tim nodded. This was better than he'd expected.

'As long as you promise to stay safe,' Larry continued. 'Keep away from Hera, she's nuts. And if you ever have troubles, make sure you come to me.' He held out his hand. 'Deal?'

Tim shook the teacher's hand with both of his.

'Deal! Thank you so much!'

'Great. Shall we go downstairs? I smell apple pie.' Larry rolled his eyes comically. 'Mmm, my favourite!' He sprang up from the chair and strode to the door. 'Your mother wouldn't believe me anyway. Sounds pretty far-fetched. A modern-day schoolboy running around in Ancient Gr–'

The teacher had just reached for the doorknob when he came to an abrupt halt. He turned slowly and Tim was shocked by the sudden change in Larry's face. It was as if he'd received horrible news or had seen a ghost.

'I just realised something,' Larry said. His jaw was rigid.

'What?' Tim asked, his fists clenching involuntarily.

'Sit down again.' Larry waited until Tim was seated, but he remained standing. 'I took the younger kids on a trip to the British Museum the other day. You know, like the one you're going on soon. I was looking at the Ancient Greek exhibits.' He paused.

'Yes?' Tim prompted.

'I didn't think anything of it at the time, but there was this strange object on display. It was a Greek pot, but not like this one.' He waved at the amphora. 'It was small. An oil flask, I think they said. A new find.'

Tim didn't see what there was to worry about, as long as it wasn't *his* vase that was locked up in a museum.

'The experts are confused,' Larry continued. 'No one knows what to make of it.'

'How come?'

Larry spoke slowly, choosing his words with care. 'There's a picture on the front. You know how the Greeks drew pictures on vases, showing people and heroes?'

Tim glanced at his vase, the one that had once imprisoned Hercules. 'Like that drawing of Hercules wrestling a bull?'

'Exactly. Well – this one's a bit unusual. It has a picture of a boy. And he's not dressed like the people in other pictures, in cloaks and tunics.' Larry's forehead creased as he spoke. 'It sounds crazy, but it looks like he's wearing a modern-day school uniform. And the boy in the picture is clinging on to a vase.'

Tim felt a tingle run down his spine, even before the teacher stopped speaking.

'I don't know what it means, but Tim … I think that boy is *you*.'

Look out for Tim's next ADVENTURE!

HOPELESS HEROES

APOLLO'S MYSTIC MESSAGE!

STELLA
TARAKSON

Sweet
Cherry

1

'Dessert's ready!' Tim Baker's mother called from the kitchen. The smell of freshly baked apple pie drifted up the stairs, through Tim's open door and into his room. Mum's too-cheery voice sounded strained and forced. Tim thought he knew why.

As far as Mum knew, he and her boyfriend Larry – an Australian who was a teacher at Tim's school – were having a man-to-man talk about how they would get along together. Mum wanted so much for Tim and the teacher to like each other. This was the first time that she'd had a boyfriend since Tim's father died. He could tell she was nervous about it. So was he.

In a way, it was true: Tim and Larry *were* working out how they would get along. What Mum didn't know, however, was how they were doing it. She didn't know that Tim had told Larry his biggest secret. She didn't know what that secret was – or even that he had one.

Tim had told Larry that he could time travel to and from Ancient Greece. He hadn't been boasting or trying to impress the teacher. Far from it: Tim had no choice. It was either trust Larry and ask for help, or let down his friend Zoe when she needed him the most.

Zoe was the daughter of the Greek hero who'd been trapped in Mum's vase. Hercules had been imprisoned by Hera, the spiteful queen goddess of Olympus, for thousands of years until Tim accidentally broke the vase and freed him. That same vase now allowed Tim to travel through time and have adventures. But freeing the hero had angered Hera. She was determined to recapture Hercules, and didn't much like Tim and Zoe

getting in the way. Her latest punishment had been to trap Zoe in a giant puzzle prison.

Larry was the only person who could solve the puzzle and let Zoe out – so Tim had asked for his help. Luckily, the teacher turned out to be unflappable and kind of cool. Everything had been fine and 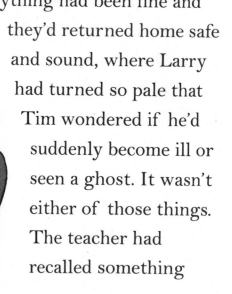 they'd returned home safe and sound, where Larry had turned so pale that Tim wondered if he'd suddenly become ill or seen a ghost. It wasn't either of those things. The teacher had recalled something he'd seen at the British Museum. Something that had the experts puzzled …

It was a recently discovered Ancient Greek oil flask. Strangely, it seemed to have a drawing of a boy wearing a modern school uniform. Knowing what he now did about Tim's adventures, Larry thought it might be a picture of Tim.

'I'm sorry, mate, but I don't think you should time travel any more,' Larry said, his green eyes glittering. 'You might be changing history – you *are* changing history. After all, if you hadn't visited the past, that flask wouldn't exist.'

Tim shrugged. 'It's only a picture on a pot.

How does that change anything?'

'The thing is, we just don't know.'
Larry perched on the edge of Tim's bed
and stretched out his long legs. 'Think of
it like this: you throw a pebble in a pond
and it makes a small splash. But it doesn't
end there. It creates ripples, and they
spread. Have you ever
heard of the butterfly
effect?'

Tim looked back
blankly. What did
butterflies have to do
with pebbles?
Or ponds, for
that matter.

'A butterfly

flaps its wings in China,' Larry said, flapping his fingers. 'A week later, a tornado hits America. Did the butterfly's wings cause the tornado?'

Tim gaped. Was the man crazy? Maybe the adventure had been too much for him!

Larry, guessing what Tim was thinking, smiled weakly. 'It's a maths idea called chaos theory. Small things can lead to big changes, in ways that are hard to predict.'

'It's only a picture—'

'A picture that shouldn't exist,' Larry cut in

firmly. 'How many times have you visited the past?'

Tim tried to do a quick calculation in his head but failed. 'Um, not many …' He scrunched his face in thought. 'I didn't see any butterflies though,' he added helpfully.

Larry blinked. 'OK … But already things have changed. And what about me? Flashing my mobile phone around like that! I shouldn't have flaunted it in the ancient world.'

'You had to,' Tim said, remembering how frightened Hera had been of the modern technology. With it, Larry had convinced the goddess that he had magical powers she couldn't hope to understand. It was only her confusion that had allowed them to escape.

'Ripples in time,' Larry said darkly. 'Tiny changes that spread and grow, over thousands of years. If you keep going back, the effect could get bigger and bigger. It could change the present in ways we'd never expect.'

'But if I'm extra careful ...'

'NO, TIM.'

Larry pressed his lips together. 'It's started already.'

'It might not be me on the flask!' Tim protested. 'Maybe you've got it wrong! You'd be spoiling everything for nothing.'

'Coffee's going cold!' Mum's voice floated up the stairs.

'Tell you what,' Larry said, standing up and walking to the door. 'You've got a trip to the British Museum next week, right? I've been rostered on to help. We'll look at the flask together. If it isn't a picture of you, well, then it might be okay.'

A week was an awfully long time to wait.

'You couldn't take me before then, could you?' Tim asked as they went down the stairs. 'Maybe this weekend?'

'Not a good idea, mate. Your mum and I aren't ready to go public yet.'

'What isn't a good idea?' Mum met them in the hallway and ushered them into the kitchen. Her brow furrowed as she spoke.

'All's good, Penny, don't worry,'
Larry reassured her. 'We've reached an
understanding.'

'Can you take me to the British
Museum this weekend, Mum?'

She shook her head as she slid a piece
of apple pie and a glass of milk before
Tim. 'I've got too much work. My
deadline's approaching. Anyway, aren't
you going with school?
Why go twice?'

She looked from Tim to Larry and back again.

Tim knew not to push it. Mum would ask too many awkward questions.

'Oh, yeah. I forgot.'

'There we are then. You can wait.' Mum nodded, satisfied. 'Do you want ice cream or custard with your pie?'

'How about both?' Larry said, and grinned.

Tim knew the teacher was trying to make him feel better. But not even ice cream and custard could calm the butterflies in his stomach.

The week passed slowly, but finally
the day of the trip arrived. Tim had to
remember to call Larry "Mr Green" in
front of the other kids – especially if
Leo the bully was around. The last thing
Tim needed was for Leo to figure out
that the teacher was seeing Tim's mother.
Tim knew from hard experience that if
Leo smelled a mystery, he wouldn't stop
prying.

Leo enjoyed upsetting Tim. He was the one who'd come up with the annoying nickname "Cinderella". All because Tim was lumbered with the housework! It wasn't his fault Mum had to work two jobs, leaving him to do the chores.

'Hey everyone, watch. What's this?' Leo pulled a tissue out of his pocket and pretended to dust a sarcophagus in the

Egypt room. Heads swivelled, but Tim gritted his teeth and stared straight ahead. He could guess what was coming.

'Cinderella at home with his mummy!' Leo brayed, wobbling with mirth.

All of the kids laughed except for Tim and his best friend Ajay. 'Ignore him,' Ajay said, dark eyes flashing. 'Act like you didn't notice.'

'What's the matter?' Leo sidled up to them. 'That comment was pharaoh-nuff! *Pharaoh*-nuff! Get it? Like *fair enough*?

HAH!'

Ajay fixed Leo with a hard stare. 'I wouldn't get too close to that mummy if I were you,' he said, his voice deadpan. 'There's a curse on it. Last time someone touched it, their freckles fell off.'

Leo's hand automatically strayed to his cheek, but then he scowled. 'Yeah, very funny. You need to watch yourself before someone fixes you up.'

'Come on, boys, keep moving.' Their class teacher Miss Omiros shooed them along as Larry strode ahead. 'There's a lot to get through.'

Normally Tim would be interested in everything, but today he only had eyes for Greek pottery. He passed the Egyptian and Assyrian exhibits with barely a glance. Finally, they reached the room with the Greek vases. Tim snapped his head around, trying to take it all in at once. He only succeeded in making himself dizzy.

Larry coughed and caught his eye. The teacher nodded towards a glass cabinet in the centre of the room. Folding his arms casually, Larry moved behind Tim as he crossed to the display. There, on a high shelf, was a slender flask. Tim had to stand on his toes to get a better look.

Only about thirty centimetres tall, it was much smaller than his magic vase. The flask had a single loop-shaped handle and a narrow neck. A band of intricate decorations circled the flask, but Tim's gaze shot straight to the figure etched on the white background. His eyes bulged.

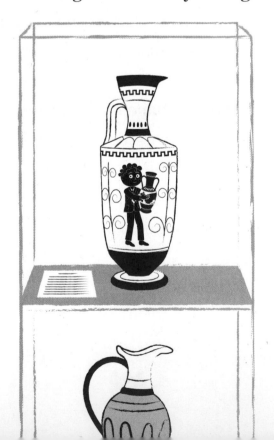

THE BOY WAS DRESSED EXACTLY LIKE HIM.

Tim glanced down at his school uniform: trousers, shirt, blazer, tie. Nobody in Ancient Greece dressed like that. They believed only barbarians wore trousers. And ties – surely they hadn't even been invented yet.

Most worrying was the fact that the boy was holding a vase. It was identical to Tim's, right down to the picture of Hercules wrestling a bull on the front.

Larry pointed at a printed sheet of paper next to the flask. Tim craned his neck for a closer look.

UNSOLVED MYSTERY

This new find has stirred a great deal
of interest amongst archaeologists.
The white-ground lekythos — or
oil flask — is typical of the type
used as grave gifts in Attica. Dated
circa 540-480 BC, this flask is
unusual in its decoration. Most
depict burial rites and the journey
to the afterlife of the deceased.
This figure, however, seems to be
wearing modern dress. Tagged the
Time Traveller's Flask, the find
has sparked debate. Accusations
of hoaxes have been made, yet all
analyses so far indicate that this is a
genuine article.

Gulping, Tim turned away. The words "grave gifts" and "burial rites" echoed through his skull like a tolling bell.

'Whaddya looking at, Cinderella?' Leo asked, pushing in front of Tim to see what had caught his interest.

'I'd get rid of those jelly beans quick smart if I were you, Leo,' Larry said, without even glancing at the boy. 'If I see you sneak one out of your pocket again, I'll confiscate the whole bag.'

Leo scuttled away but Tim felt no sense of triumph. He looked at the teacher, who frowned and shook his head.

'See what I mean? It's you.' Larry spoke under his breath, so that nobody else could hear.

'I've changed the past,' Tim whispered. Images of butterflies and tornadoes spun through his head.

'I'm afraid so,' Larry said, frowning.

Suddenly a thought occurred to Tim and he gasped. Larry looked at him questioningly.

'The vase that Hera trapped Hercules in had his picture on it. This has my picture on it …' Tim swallowed as he put two and two together. 'Does that mean … Is Hera after *me* now?'

HOPELESS HEROES

To download Hopeless Heroes

ACTIVITIES
AND
POSTERS

visit:
www.sweetcherrypublishing.com/resources

Sweet Cherry